The Upside-Down Day

Beverly Lewis

Beverly Lewis Books for Young Readers

PICTURE BOOKS

Annika's Secret Wish • *In Jesse's Shoes*
Just Like Mama • *What Is God Like?*
What Is Heaven Like?

THE CUL-DE-SAC KIDS

The Double Dabble Surprise
The Chicken Pox Panic
The Crazy Christmas Angel Mystery
No Grown-ups Allowed
Frog Power
The Mystery of Case D. Luc
The Stinky Sneakers Mystery
Pickle Pizza
Mailbox Mania
The Mudhole Mystery
Fiddlesticks
The Crabby Cat Caper
Tarantula Toes
Green Gravy
Backyard Bandit Mystery
Tree House Trouble
The Creepy Sleep-Over
The Great TV Turn-Off
Piggy Party
The Granny Game
Mystery Mutt
Big Bad Beans
The Upside-Down Day
The Midnight Mystery

Katie and Jake and the Haircut Mistake

www.BeverlyLewis.com

THE CUL-DE-SAC KIDS

The Upside-Down Day

·

Beverly Lewis

BETHANY HOUSE PUBLISHERS
MINNEAPOLIS, MINNESOTA 55438

© 2001 by Beverly Lewis

Published by Bethany House Publishers
11400 Hampshire Avenue South
Bloomington, Minnesota 55438
www.bethanyhouse.com

Bethany House Publishers is a division of
Baker Publishing Group, Grand Rapids, MI

Printed in the United States of America by
Bethany Press International, Bloomington, MN

ISBN 978-0-7642-2128-6

Library of Congress Cataloging-in-Publication Data
    Lewis, Beverly.
    The upside-down day / by Beverly Lewis.
        p.   cm.—(The cul-de-sac kids ; 23)
    Summary: During School Spirit Week, the new girl in school challenges
the Cul-de-sac Kids to guess her secret.
    ISBN 0-7642-2128-0 (pbk.)
    [1. Schools—fiction. 2. Secrets—fiction.] I. Title.
PZ7.L58464 Up   2001
[Fic]—dc21   00-011571

Cover illustration by Paul Turnbaugh
Cover design by Lookout Design, Inc.
Text Illustrations by Janet Huntington

15 16 17 18 19 20 21   20 19 18 17 16 15 14

To Amy, my niece,
who played a trick
on Barbara Birch's fourth-grade class
at Pikes Peak Elementary School.

THE CUL-DE-SAC KIDS

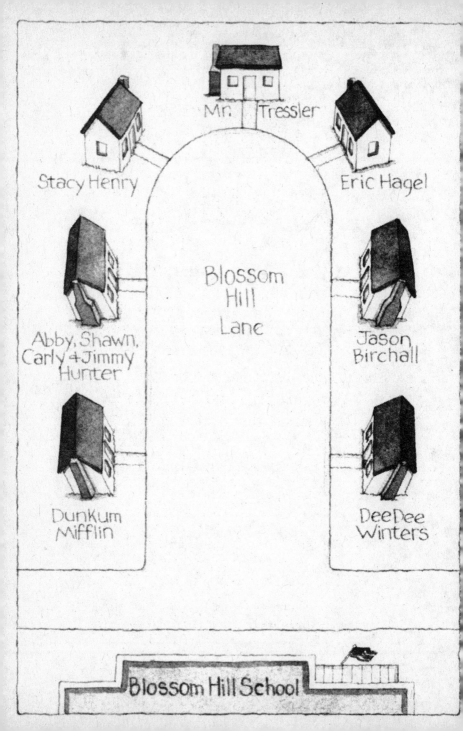

ONE

School Spirit Day was coming to Blossom Hill School.

"We're going to have so much fun," said Abby Hunter. She and her friend Stacy Henry hurried down the cul-de-sac together.

Stacy grinned. "I've got *lots* of school spirit," she said.

"Remember the fun we had last year?" said Abby.

"Sure do," Stacy said, skipping along.

"The teachers did real silly things," Abby said.

"I wonder what Miss Hershey will do," Stacy said.

Abby was sure Miss Hershey would make things interesting. "I can't wait to find out," she replied.

★　★　★

The Cul-de-sac Kids walked to school together every day. Rain or shine.

But today, something was different.

Abby noticed a girl sitting on Dunkum Mifflin's porch swing. She had long, brown hair. Her eyes were closed, and a golden Labrador dog sat nearby. "Who's that?" Abby whispered to Stacy.

Stacy shook her head. "I've never seen her before."

Abby wondered. "Is she asleep on Dunkum's porch?" she asked more softly.

"I can't tell if she's asleep or not," Stacy replied.

Abby inched closer. "Hello?" she called to the girl.

"Hello, yourself," the girl said. But her eyes were still closed. "You're Abby Hunter, right?"

How does she know? Abby wondered.

"Wow! How did you DO that?" Stacy blurted out.

The girl's eyes opened, but they stared straight ahead. "Dunkum said you'd show up soon. That's how."

Abby looked at the girl. She looked at the dog. She looked back at the girl. *She's blind*, Abby decided. *And whoever she is, she knows Dunkum. But . . . she can't see.*

"What's *your* name?" asked Abby.

"Ellen Mifflin. I'm Dunkum's cousin. This is my guide dog, Honey."

"So . . . are you visiting Dunkum?" Abby asked.

"I'm staying for a couple of months. My dad is overseas with his job."

"Hey, that's great," Abby said. "We need more girls in the Cul-de-sac Kids club."

"Sure do!" agreed Stacy.

"What's a Cul-de-sac Kids club?" asked Ellen.

"Well, we live on a cul-de-sac. So we have a Cul-de-sac Kids club," Abby explained.

"Sounds like fun," said Ellen. "How many girls?"

"Counting you, there are five. You, me, my sister, Carly, Dee Dee Winters, and Stacy Henry." Abby pulled her friend closer. "Stacy's right here beside me."

"Hi, Stacy," said Ellen with a smile.

"Welcome to Blossom Hill Lane," Stacy said.

Just then, Dunkum leaped out the door. He aimed his basketball at the hoop. He shot. *Swish*. Right through!

"Hi, Abby and Stacy. Did you meet my cousin?" He dribbled the ball behind his back. He loved to show off.

"Sure did," Abby said. "Why didn't you tell us she was coming?"

"You needed another mystery to solve," Dunkum said.

Abby grinned. Dunkum knew she liked a good mystery.

"Speaking of mysteries, are you finished reading *Mystery History* yet?" Abby asked Dunkum.

"Is that all you care about—reading

and writing?" Dunkum teased.

"That, and solving mysteries—don't forget!" Abby added. "So did you finish my book or not?"

"Yep, I'll go get it for you." Dunkum disappeared into the house.

Ellen giggled. "Dunkum forgets stuff. I bet he even forgot to tell you I was coming."

The girls laughed. Ellen was right.

In a flash, Dunkum was back with Abby's book.

Just then, down the street someone hollered, "Wait for us!"

Abby turned to look. The rest of the Cul-de-sac Kids were on their way.

"Here come the rest of the kids," said Abby.

Abby's little sister, Carly, and little brother Jimmy ran down the sidewalk. "Nice doggie!" Carly cried when she spied Honey.

"Ellen, meet my sister and brother, Carly and Jimmy," said Abby.

"Hi, Ellen, what's your doggie's name?" Carly asked.

"Hi, Carly." Ellen laughed. "I call my dog Honey."

"I like puppy dogs," said Jimmy, petting Honey.

Eric Hagel came running, too. "Better hurry, or we'll be late for school," he said.

"Relax, Eric," said Dunkum. "Give Jason a chance to catch up."

Jason Birchall ran along behind Eric.

Soon, Abby's Korean brother Shawn came down Blossom Hill Lane. "I am very sorry to be late." It sounded like *velly* sorry.

"Nobody's late," Dunkum said, shooting one more basket.

But Dunkum's mom dashed across the lawn. "*I'm* late! I must enroll Ellen before she can attend school."

"Oops, I almost forgot," Dunkum said.

The girls covered their mouths, giggling.

"What's so funny?" Dunkum asked.

Abby swallowed another giggle. "Oh, nothing," she said.

Eric tossed the basketball to Jason.

Jason bounced the ball slowly. He stared at Ellen and Honey. "Who's the new girl?" he asked.

Dunkum sounded like he was making a speech. "Everybody, meet my cousin Ellen. Ellen, meet Eric Hagel, Shawn Hunter, and Jason Birchall."

"Now we *are* gonna be late!" Eric complained.

The kids turned and hurried down the walk.

Jason watched Honey guide Ellen forward. "How will the dog know when to cross the street?" he asked.

"She's trained to listen for cars," Dunkum said. "Just watch when we get to the curb."

Abby's sister, Carly, suddenly dropped her show-and-tell. It was a giant green lizard puppet with a long tail.

Honey began barking loudly.

Ellen frowned and stopped walking.

"What's wrong with Honey?" She tightened her hold on the harness.

"It's OK, Ellen," said Dunkum. "It's just Carly's ugly puppet."

"She's *not* ugly!" shouted Carly.

Dunkum chuckled. "It's a *she*?"

"God made girl lizards, too," Carly said, grinning.

"You're right," said Dunkum. "I forgot." He circled the girls, bouncing the ball.

The Cul-de-sac Kids laughed as they reached the end of the block.

Honey led Ellen to the curb. They waited for a moment. A car passed by slowly, and Honey stepped back. Ellen did, too.

Soon it was safe. The dog guided Ellen across the street to school.

"Wow," said Carly and Dee Dee.

"Honey's cool," said Eric.

Dunkum's mother took Ellen and her dog to the school office. The kids yelled their good-byes. They promised to meet at recess.

"Two things will be exciting this week,"

Abby said. "One is School Spirit Day. The second thing is having a dog for a class-mate."

"No kidding," said Stacy. Her eyes were bright.

Abby could hardly wait for school to start!

TWO

Miss Hershey was seating a girl with red pigtails.

"Looks like we have *another* new girl," Abby said. She tried not to stare.

Stacy opened her desk behind Abby's.

Abby watched her friend dig through her desk. "What are you looking for?" she asked.

"A piece of paper," Stacy muttered. She closed her desk quickly.

Abby ripped a page from her notebook. "Here." She gave the paper to Stacy.

Stacy began to draw a secret message for the new girl. The letters and numbers spelled out something special.

Well + come 2 R Class

"Will you take this to the new girl?" she asked.

"*You* take it. Don't be shy," Abby said. She pushed the note back into Stacy's hand.

Stacy wrinkled her face. Then she crept across the room. She slid the note onto the new girl's desk. And she hurried back to her own desk.

Abby and Stacy watched the new girl open the note. She gave them a creepy smile.

Stacy smiled back. Abby didn't know whether to smile or frown.

Jason plopped down on Abby's desk. "Hey, look at that. The new girl's got red pigtails."

"So what?" said Abby.

"Don't you see? Her hair's too short for pigtails," Jason joked. "They stick straight out."

"Be nice," Abby said. "She's new. Besides, we should treat others the way *we* want to be treated."

Jason crossed his eyes and scrunched up his face.

Rrrinng! The last bell before school started.

Miss Hershey's students scrambled to their seats. She called roll. Then she asked the new girl to stand and say her name.

"I'm Leslie Groff," said the girl. She sat down real fast.

Abby thought Leslie must surely be in the wrong class. Leslie was way too short for their grade.

★ ★ ★

After spelling class, Ellen and her guide dog showed up.

Miss Hershey assigned a desk to Ellen in the back of the room. Honey could stretch out there.

Abby couldn't help staring at Honey. Her classmates kept looking at the beautiful dog, too.

"Students, please face the front," Miss

Hershey said several times during math.

When it was time for reading, Leslie Groff sat beside Abby. Halfway through the story, she whispered, "I have a secret."

Abby looked at her. "A secret? What is it?"

"Can't tell," she whispered.

"Then let me guess," Abby said.

"You'll never guess in a trillion and one years."

A mystery! Abby was ready for the challenge. Her mind was racing. She *had* to solve it . . . whatever the mystery was!

At recess, Abby played with the other Cul-de-sac Kids. They gathered near the slide and took turns petting Honey. Abby asked, "What could Leslie's secret be?"

Dunkum had an idea. "Maybe she's a cousin to Anne of Green Gables. *She* had red hair, too."

They cracked up, laughing.

"Leslie looks like a second grader to me. She probably skipped a grade," said Eric.

"I think so, too!" said Abby. "That's got to be her secret."

Ellen sat on the end of the slide. Honey was licking her hand. "Where's Leslie now?" Ellen asked.

"She stayed inside with Miss Hershey," Jason said. Then he doubled over, laughing hard. "Leslie's short, skinny pigtails match her legs!"

Abby didn't think it was funny. "Jason, what about the Golden Rule?"

"That's right," said Dunkum. "Besides, some kids can't help being skinny."

"And some kids can't help being *girls*!" joked Jason.

"Come on, Jason, let's play ball," Dunkum suggested. "The girls are gonna clobber you!"

Eric smiled at Abby. "Jason didn't really mean it, you know." He ran off to join the boys.

Ellen giggled. "Uh-oh, Abby. Eric *likes* you."

"Why do you think that?" asked Abby.

"I just do," said Ellen.

The recess bell rang.

On the way inside, Ellen promised to show Abby and Stacy her Braille machine. "It makes little dots stick up off the paper. I can feel each dot with my fingers," Ellen explained. "That's how I read."

"It's like a secret code," Abby said. "Which reminds me of Leslie Groff. I *have* to figure out her secret!"

THREE

The next day, Abby's father woke her. "Hurry, Abby. You overslept!"

She sat up in bed and rubbed her eyes. "Wha-at?"

"Fifteen minutes before breakfast," her father said. "Hurry, you'll be late for school!"

Abby tossed off the covers. She threw on a blouse and pants. She swished a toothbrush over her teeth and brushed her hair. Grabbing *Mystery History*, she was off to breakfast.

But the kitchen was empty.

"Daddy?"

"I'm in here," he called from his study.

"Where *is* everybody?" she asked.

He looked at his watch. "Well, my goodness! It's only six o'clock."

"Da-a-ddy!" Abby squealed. "You tricked me."

He gave her a bear hug. "Happy School Spirit Day, honey."

"You're getting me ready for the fun at school, right?"

Her father winked, wearing a big smile.

Then Abby had an idea.

She tiptoed to her sister's room. "Psst, Carly!"

Carly rolled over in bed. She rubbed her eyes and stretched.

Abby tried to sound serious. "If you don't hurry, you'll be late for school."

Carly looked at her big sister already dressed for school. She jumped out of bed. Her foot stuck in the covers. Carly rolled, falling to the floor. *Thud!*

"Here, I'll help you." Abby untangled the covers for Carly. She pulled her foot out, too. All the while, she tried not to burst out laughing.

While her sister hurried to the bathroom, Abby hid behind the bedroom door. Soon she heard Carly rush off to the kitchen.

Things were very quiet. But only for a moment.

"Abby!" wailed Carly. "No one's up! What's going on?"

Abby inched out of hiding. "Happy School Spirit Day!" she said.

"But this isn't school," Carly said. "This is our home." So she crawled back into her unmade bed. "You'll be sorry for this," she grumbled.

"Aw, don't be mad," said Abby. "Now you'll have time to make your bed and pick up your room. *Before* school starts."

"Hey, you're not the boss!" said Carly. She threw her pillow at Abby.

Abby ran to her own room and slammed the door. Carly chased her. She pounded on Abby's door.

"What's all the racket?" Mother called sleepily.

Abby tried not to giggle. She secretly blamed Carly for all the noise.

"Please tell your sister to be quieter," Mother said.

"I will," Abby called back with a grin.

★ ★ ★

At school, Miss Hershey was wearing a purple suit. Her jacket was on backward. Her earrings were clipped on backward, too. Even the day's schedule was written on the chalkboard backward.

Abby looked hard at the jumbled words. *Hoo-ray!* Reading class was first.

"Happy School Spirit Day," Miss Hershey told the class. "For several months now, we've been reading mysteries. All of you are learning to gather clues." She made her voice sound a little sneaky. "So . . . pay very close attention. You never know where a mystery might pop up."

Abby wondered about Leslie Groff's secret. Before class, Leslie had dropped a note on Abby's desk. Abby pulled it out and read it again. It was in a code, with pictures and words mixed up.

"Class, we're having art first today," their teacher said.

Jason raised his hand. "I don't get it. The schedule says reading class is first."

Miss Hershey nodded. "Just remember—anything can happen today." There was that mystery sound in her voice again.

Abby was all ears. She listened carefully when Miss Hershey assigned them to tables.

She hid her book under the table during art. She couldn't wait to read the last chapter of *Mystery History*.

Leslie sat on the other side of the table. "What are you doing?" she asked.

Abby held up the book. "I'm going to guess your secret. *This* will help me."

"Do you really think so?" asked Leslie. She had a funny look in her eyes.

"Yep."

2 the girl who ♡s mysteries.

U guess M + 🖐 C + cret?

👁 give U till the N + 2 of school 2 t day.

6 hours, not counting lunch.

LG

"How would you like one clue?" Leslie asked.

"Double dabble good!" said Abby. She was ready.

Leslie's smile was sneaky. "OK, here goes." She leaned closer.

Abby closed her book. She sat up straight.

"Remember, things aren't always as they seem," Leslie whispered.

That's not a clue, Abby thought. "Give me a better one," she said.

"My father is a king." Leslie's voice was sly. "How's that for a clue?"

"But is it true?" asked Abby.

"Maybe, maybe not," said Leslie.

Abby knew about presidents. But kings and queens? Who was this girl trying to fool?

★ ★ ★

After art, Miss Hershey announced a special reading assignment. "I am handing out a test. You must complete it before math class."

Tests were icksville for Abby. She waved her pencil at Leslie Groff. Leslie smiled back. But it was another sneaky smile. *What could Leslie's secret be?* Abby wondered.

Miss Hershey gave directions. "Remember, read all the questions first."

Abby glanced back at Ellen. Honey was taking a nap at Ellen's feet. Abby got up to sharpen her pencil. She passed Ellen's desk on the way. She peeked at Ellen's test. *So this is Braille*, she thought.

The classroom was suddenly very quiet. Everyone was working hard on the tests.

Soon, Honey was guiding Ellen to Miss Hershey's desk.

She can't be finished yet, thought Abby. She looked at her own paper. She was only on number seven.

A few minutes later, Leslie Groff was finished. Then Dunkum and Stacy.

Abby looked around the room. She was getting worried. *Something's wrong*, she thought. *Very wrong!*

FOUR

Abby noticed Jason still writing his test.

Good, she thought, *I'm not the only one.*

Miss Hershey turned away from the chalkboard. "For students who are still working, remember to read *all* questions first," she reminded them.

Abby put her pencil down and read each question. The last question was: If you have read all the questions, please write only your name, address, and telephone number at the bottom of this page. Then turn in the test.

Very tricky, Abby thought. *I didn't follow directions.*

Quickly, she wrote her name, address, and telephone number at the bottom of the page. Then she scooted down in her seat.

"What are you doing?" Stacy whispered behind Abby.

"I feel like crawling under my desk," she whispered back. "I'm so embarrassed."

Then Abby heard Miss Hershey's voice. "Will you please give Jason a hint about the test, Abby?"

Her mouth was dry as if she'd eaten chalk. Dry and yucky.

She looked at Jason. *Poor Jason. He's still working.*

Abby's voice cracked as she said, "Don't write anything until you read the whole page."

Jason twirled his pencil. He read to the bottom of the test. Suddenly, his face turned Christmas red. "Oh, *now* I get it," he said. "Good trick, Miss Hershey."

The class howled with laughter, including Jason.

What a double dabble good joke!

Miss Hershey glanced around the

room. "Now, listen very carefully. Following directions is a good thing to do every day. Not only School Spirit Day." With that, the teacher winked at Leslie.

Abby blinked. She turned around. "Did you see that?" she asked Stacy.

Stacy nodded. "Something's up."

"OK, it's time for some riddle fun," said Miss Hershey. "Anyone?"

Dunkum raised his hand. "*I've* got a riddle. What do you get when you cross a duck with a cow?"

"Anyone know?" Miss Hershey asked, looking around.

No one answered.

"Quackers and milk!" said Dunkum with glee.

Everyone clapped.

"Yay, Dunkum!" shouted Jason.

"Go, Dunkum!" said Eric more softly.

Ellen raised her hand next.

"Yes?" Miss Hershey said.

Ellen smiled so big, her face seemed to light up. "What is the beginning of eternity, the end of time and space, the beginning of every end, and the end of every race?" she asked.

Stacy whispered, "What a mouthful."

Miss Hershey nodded. "That's an excellent question, Ellen. Does anyone know the answer?"

The students looked puzzled.

At last, Jason raised his hand.

"Go ahead, Jason," Miss Hershey said.

He grinned and shook his head. "Sorry," he said. "I don't know the answer. I can't even figure out the question!"

The kids were laughing again.

Miss Hershey looked at Ellen. "I believe you've stumped us. Please tell us the answer."

"The answer is the letter E," Ellen replied.

The kids clapped for Ellen's riddle. Abby clapped extra hard.

Jason raised his hand again. He still looked confused. "I don't get it," he admitted.

Leslie giggled.

Miss Hershey explained. "E begins the

words *eternity* and *end*. And E ends the words *time, space*, and *race*."

Jason was jiving at his desk. "Oh, yeah!" he said. "Very cool."

Leslie raised her hand. "*I* have a riddle, too."

"Yes, Leslie?" Miss Hershey said.

"If all of you lived to be a trillion and one years old, you could never guess my secret."

Never? Abby held her breath.

She thought about Leslie's first clue, earlier today. Many kings and queens lived in England, long ago. Maybe that *was* a good clue after all. Abby waved her hand high. "Are you from England, and did you skip second grade?" she asked.

"Nope to both guesses," Leslie said. Her grin turned from sneaky to unkind.

Time was ticking away. Abby had less than six hours now. And she didn't like it. Not one bit.

FIVE

Time for lunch.

Abby slipped into line with Stacy. Jason cut in line behind her. Leslie squealed.

In a flash, Miss Hershey pulled Jason out of line. The rest of the class headed off to lunch.

The older Cul-de-sac Kids always ate together at school. Today, Jason came in five minutes late. He plodded across the floor to their table. "I got in trouble," he explained. "All because Leslie Groff screamed. She got me in trouble!"

Jason scooted into the seat and opened

his lunch. He poked his nose inside, then slammed the sack shut. "Anybody want to trade?" he pleaded.

"What's in there?" Dunkum asked.

"Rabbit food," Jason replied. He pulled a face.

Dunkum held out his hand for Jason's carrot and celery sticks. "I'll trade your veggies for my orange pieces."

"It's a deal," Jason said.

Next thing, all the kids started trading food. Eric even gave away his chocolate chip cookie. To Abby.

Abby was double dabble glad about that. "Thanks, Eric." She wondered if Ellen was right about Eric. Maybe he *did* like her extra-special.

Well, Abby liked him, too. They went to the same church and both liked mystery books. Besides that, Eric's mom made great chocolate chip cookies. "Yum," she said, enjoying every bite.

★ ★ ★

The kids chattered off and on about Leslie.

"Any ideas about her secret?" Eric asked Abby.

Abby shook her head. "Not yet."

"I think Leslie *looks* like a second grader," Stacy said. "But nothing like a princess."

"She doesn't act like royalty," Jason said. He was being more serious now.

Abby scratched her head. "So . . . what could the secret be?"

"Maybe she has a twin sister," suggested Jason. "And her twin got all the hair."

The kids laughed. A piece of Dunkum's sandwich flew out of his mouth.

The kids cackled some more.

"Maybe she's a friend of Miss Hershey," said Stacy.

"Or a neighbor," said Shawn.

"Could Leslie be Miss Hershey's relative?" Jason asked.

"I saw Miss Hershey wink at Leslie. Abby saw it, too," Stacy said.

Abby nodded. "There's something really weird going on."

"Leslie doesn't look like Miss Hershey at all," said Dunkum.

"Yeah, and Miss Hershey isn't a queen," said Jason. "And her husband can't be a king—"

"Because Miss Hershey isn't married!" Abby broke in.

"Hey. . . . Maybe the king rules on a secret island somewhere," said Eric.

"Yeah, *right*," Abby replied. "This is getting us nowhere. We need solid clues."

Ellen had an idea. "Maybe there isn't any secret. Maybe *that's* the secret."

Jason sputtered between apple bites. "Leslie better not set us up for nothing."

"Jason's right," Abby said. "That would be a mean trick."

Just then, Leslie approached their table. She was licking a pink lollipop. "What's Jason right about?" She glared at him.

The Cul-de-sac Kids were silent.

SIX

Leslie repeated her question. "Are you going to tell me or not? What's Jason right about?"

Jason ignored her. He slurped on his apple and spit out the seeds. Then he stuffed them into his shirt pocket.

Abby giggled about the seeds.

Without blinking, he said, "You never know when I might get hungry."

The kids roared with laughter.

Leslie's face turned red. "You're a big show-off!"

"*You* can't call him that," Dunkum scolded.

"And why not?" Leslie demanded, her hands on her hips.

Dunkum scowled at Leslie.

She began to squirm and opened her mouth to say something. But the lunch-room teacher marched over to their table. All of them were sent out for recess.

But Leslie didn't head for the playground. She walked back toward the classroom.

Where's she going? Abby wondered. She wanted to follow Leslie, but her friends called to her from the doorway.

"OK, I'm coming!" Abby said.

★ ★ ★

Outside, Abby and Stacy hung upside down from the monkey bars. Ellen's guide dog, Honey, rested in the sand nearby.

Abby kept her eyes on Ellen, who swung straight across the bars. "You're good at that," she said.

"Thanks," Ellen replied.

"I've never known a blind person before," Stacy said. "I wondered what you were like."

Ellen swung on the bars. "I'm no different than anybody else."

Abby thought about that. "Your riddle was terrific," she said. "Did you make it up?"

Ellen dropped down from the bars. "I listen to the radio and TV a lot. If I hear something once, I never forget it."

"That's so cool," Stacy whispered.

"Can you keep a secret?" Abby asked.

"Sure," both girls answered.

"I'm going to play a joke on Miss Hershey."

"You are?" Stacy whispered. She moved closer to Abby. "Tell us more."

"I'm going to make the whole class disappear."

Ellen coughed. "How?"

"During library, when Miss Hershey has a break, I'll ask the librarian to tell the class about it. Then, during social studies, I'll see if the principal will page Miss Hershey. When she gets back from the office—*poof!* The whole class just disappeared to the library!"

"Will the principal and librarian help you?" asked Ellen.

"I think so," Abby said. "Mr. Romerez, the librarian, is a friend of my dad. And Mrs. Millar teaches Sunday school at our church. She likes a good practical joke. I'm sure she'll help me play a trick on Miss Hershey."

"Your plan sounds great," said Ellen. "I hope it works."

"Too bad we won't get to see Miss Hershey's face!" Stacy said.

When the kids filed in from recess, Leslie Groff was sliding her desk close to the teacher's.

Now what's she doing? Abby wondered. She picked up her pencil and headed for the pencil sharpener.

When she walked past Ellen's desk, Ellen touched her arm. "Abby, please bring Leslie here to me," she said.

Abby looked startled. "How did you know it was me?"

"Oh, by the way you smell," Ellen said, a big smile on her face. "And . . . that's a *good* thing."

Amazing! thought Abby. She hurried to get Leslie before the bell rang. And before time for library.

"Hey, Leslie," said Ellen. She stretched her hand out. "I didn't meet you yesterday. I'm Ellen Mifflin. I guess we should stick together, since we're the new girls, right?"

Leslie was silent at first. Then she said, "But we don't *have* to, do we?"

Abby studied Leslie. *God's Word teaches us to love each other, but some people are harder to love. Leslie Groff is one of them. What* is *her problem? And what is her secret?*

Ellen didn't seem to mind Leslie's rudeness. "Maybe we could play together at recess," she suggested.

"Maybe," Leslie replied. She tapped Ellen's hand. "There, I gave you five."

Will Leslie really go outside for the last recess? Abby wondered. *Why did she stay inside, anyway? Was she allergic to the sun or something?* Abby had read about kids like that. But, no, that couldn't be Leslie's secret.

What about her crazy story? Was *her father really a king?* Abby doubted it. Leslie didn't act very much like a princess.

The whole thing must be a lie, Abby decided. She would watch Leslie even more closely. Every move and every word.

Like a good detective.

SEVEN

In the library, Abby whispered her secret plan. Both the librarian and the principal agreed to help the class disappear. Just as she hoped!

Abby would hide in the closet while the class tiptoed to the library. She couldn't wait to see Miss Hershey's face.

So, the secret was set.

★ ★ ★

During social studies, Mrs. Millar, the principal, called Miss Hershey over the intercom. "Please come to the office, Miss Hershey," the principal said.

"I'll be right there," Miss Hershey replied. She told the class to keep busy. "No visiting with friends," she said. Then she left for the office. "I'll return in a minute."

The second she was gone, the entire class tiptoed to the library.

All but Abby. She sneaked to the closet and left the door open just a crack. Perfect!

Soon Miss Hershey returned. "Oh, my!" she gasped. "Where is my class?"

Abby giggled silently in the closet.

The trick worked! The teacher *was* surprised. School Spirit Day was so much fun.

While Abby was still hiding, Miss Hershey did a strange thing. She went to Leslie's desk and opened it. Out came a red coin purse. Miss Hershey slipped her hand into the pocket of her backward suit jacket.

Abby watched closely. She saw Miss Hershey put some money in Leslie's purse!

Abby leaped out of the closet. "Surprise!"

"My goodness—Abby!" Miss Hershey said, startled. "Where *is* everyone?"

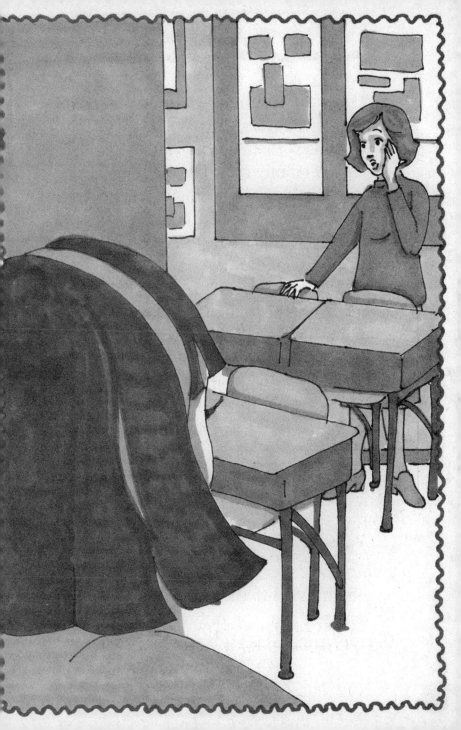

"They disappeared," shouted Abby. She clapped her hands. "It worked. We really fooled you."

"You certainly did," Miss Hershey said. "Where are they *really*?"

"In the library," Abby told her.

"Will you tell them to return to class now?" Miss Hershey asked.

Abby was eager to ask about the money. And the red coin purse. "Do you know Leslie's secret?" she asked.

Miss Hershey nodded. "Yes."

"Will she tell us today?" Abby asked.

"I think Leslie hopes someone will guess her secret," said Miss Hershey, smiling.

"This is turning into a real mystery," Abby said.

But Miss Hershey said no more.

Abby scratched her head. What was going on?

She hurried to the office. The principal let her talk over the intercom. "Operation Disappearing Class is a success. Miss Hershey's students, please return to your classroom."

Mrs. Millar patted Abby's shoulder. "School Spirit Day comes just once a year. Back to work now."

But it was already time for afternoon recess. Miss Hershey's classroom door swung wide. Kids dashed out to the playground.

Leslie ran outside, too.

"Will we find out your secret today?" Abby asked her.

Leslie ran to the swings. She shouted over her shoulder, "Someone has to guess it first! And you don't have much time left."

Leslie's answer bugged Abby. She wanted to know the secret *now*!

Ellen was playing on the monkey bars. Her guide dog waited in the sand below. While Leslie was swinging, Ellen said, "I think I know Leslie's secret."

Abby stared at her. "You do?"

"Give us a clue, OK?" Stacy begged.

"Just keep your eyes on Leslie," Ellen

said. "That's all I'm saying."

"But we *are* watching," Stacy insisted. "All the time!"

"Yeah," Abby said. "I'm tired of watching her." She wondered about Miss Hershey's actions while Abby was hiding in the closet.

"How do you know Leslie's secret?" asked Stacy.

Ellen laughed. "I guess my insight comes in handy sometimes."

They ran to the swings and played.

Then Ellen had an idea. "Let's play Twenty Questions with Leslie," she said.

"Double dabble good idea!" exclaimed Abby. "Maybe we'll get some more clues!" She turned toward Leslie's swing.

But Leslie had vanished!

"Leslie disappeared," said Abby, looking all around.

"Hey, look over there," said Stacy. "I see her."

"Leslie's running races with the boys," said Abby.

"Come on," Ellen said. "Honey needs to walk."

"OK," Abby said.

Dunkum and Eric were squatting in their get-set-go positions.

Jason yelled, "Are you ready?"

The boys shouted they were.

Abby could hardly keep her own secret inside. She had to tell Stacy and Ellen. "I saw something while I was hiding."

"Something in the closet?" Ellen asked.

"No, something *outside* the closet. Just listen to this. Miss Hershey put some money in Leslie's coin purse."

"Wha-at?" Stacy said.

"When I hid in the closet, I saw Miss Hershey open Leslie's desk," Abby explained.

"This is weird stuff," Stacy said.

"What was Miss Hershey doing in the new girl's purse?" Ellen asked.

"How should I know?" Abby said. "It's very strange."

The girls watched the races. Soon, Abby's eyes grew wide. Leslie was ahead of the boys! Abby described the entire scene to Ellen.

"Well, that fits," Ellen said softly. "Leslie really likes to show off."

Abby wished she knew *everything* Ellen knew about Leslie. She closed her eyes and pretended to be blind.

She listened. The sounds seemed sharper all around her.

She sniffed. The smells seemed stronger, too.

Suddenly, she heard yelling. She opened her eyes. It was Jason. He was chasing Leslie across the soccer field.

Abby blinked twice. She'd never seen him run so fast.

What was happening?

EIGHT

Abby stared across the playground. *This is crazy*, she thought.

Jason was running after Leslie! He was huffing and puffing. His hair was flying with every bounce.

But Leslie was far ahead of him.

Abby shouted, "Look at Jason go!"

Br-r-ring! The recess bell rang.

Jason chased Leslie around the playground and back to the school door. She raced through the door, past kids in line.

"I'm going to get that girl," Jason hollered, wiping his face.

"What did she do?" Abby asked.

"She called me a show-off again," he bellowed. "She's got no right."

Later, in the girls' bathroom, Leslie complained about Jason. "He's so hyper. Never sits still," she told Stacy and Abby.

"Oh, that's just Jason," Abby said.

Leslie pulled hard on her stubby pigtails. "How can you *say* that? He's disgusting!"

"Jason's our friend," Stacy spoke up.

"Yeah, and it doesn't make any difference to us if he's hyper."

Stacy stepped forward. "It's what's inside that counts. Think about it, Leslie Groff!" she said.

Leslie's mouth dropped open. "I thought you were *shy*." She popped some candy in her mouth and left.

"Way to go, Stacy!" Abby said. "I didn't think you'd ever talk to her like that!"

Stacy blushed. "I hope she's not mad. I didn't want to be mean."

"You were just telling the truth," Abby said. "I don't think you can be mean. You're the nicest person I know!"

Stacy's face grew red again. "I try to live the way God wants me to."

"It would be nice if everybody did that," said Abby.

Back in the room, Stacy and Abby took their seats. Miss Hershey asked the class to write their numbers. "To 300," she said.

Abby gulped. *We won't get done before the end of the day*, she thought. *And I still haven't figured out Leslie's secret.*

She started writing. 1, 2, 3, 4 . . .

Abby looked at Leslie. 23, 24, 25 . . .

Dunkum sneezed. 48, 49, 50 . . .

Eric dropped his pencil. 76, 77, 78 . . .

Abby was up to 153 when Miss Hershey announced, "OK, class. Stop writing. How many of you wrote two, three, zero, zero?" She wrote the number on the board.

Dunkum said, "We weren't supposed to write the numbers *up to* 300. You wanted us to write 2 . . . 3 . . . 0 . . . 0. Two thousand three hundred."

Abby groaned. Miss Hershey had tricked them again!

"You keep fooling us," said Jason.

"What fun," said Leslie.

Abby looked at the clock. Almost time to go home. She wasn't even close to figuring out Leslie's secret.

Abby raised her hand. "May we play Twenty Questions until we guess Leslie's secret? The bell's going to ring soon."

Miss Hershey turned to Leslie, who hopped up to the front of the room.

"Who's first?" Leslie asked.

Four hands popped up.

Dunkum asked, "Are you an alien?"

"Good guess," whispered Abby.

Leslie laughed. She shook her head. Her stubby pigtails poked out farther than ever.

Jason was next. "Are you a twin?"

Abby held her breath. Whew! Jason didn't say anything about the other twin with all the hair.

"No way," said Leslie.

Eric's hand was high. "Do you sing in the shower with a British accent?"

The kids laughed. So did Leslie.

That wasn't it.

Abby's turn. "Did Miss Hershey owe you some money?"

Leslie looked puzzled. She turned to the teacher. "How did she know?"

Abby waited. She felt like a detective close to cracking a case.

Leslie nodded. "Miss Hershey owed me some money."

"Why?" Abby asked.

"We made a deal. If the class guessed my secret before lunch, I owed her a dollar. But if no one guessed by then, she owed me," Leslie explained.

Why would the teacher make a deal like that? thought Abby.

Abby studied the new girl.

Leslie's eyes danced. She was having too much fun with this secret. Maybe she didn't want the mystery to be solved at all.

Suddenly, Honey barked loudly. She was straining on her harness. She seemed to be pulling Ellen away from the desk.

"What's wrong with Honey?" Abby asked.

Honey sniffed the air. *Woof!* She began to bark.

Then Ellen shouted, "Miss Hershey, I smell smoke!"

At that moment, the fire alarm sounded.

NINE

"Students, please line up quickly!" Miss Hershey said. The fire alarm kept ringing.

Abby was nervous. She got in line behind Ellen and her dog. Dunkum held the door.

Miss Hershey grabbed Leslie's hand as they left the classroom. She was still holding it when the line formed away from the building.

Abby watched closely. *Why would Miss Hershey hold Leslie's hand?*

"Is the school on fire?" yelled Jason.

Ellen held on to Honey's harness. "I hope not," she said.

"Just think, if the alarm hadn't sounded, Honey might've saved our lives," said Eric.

"Because Honey smelled the smoke!" said Abby.

"Wow," said Stacy. "I'm impressed."

In the front of the line, Leslie stared back at them.

But Abby smiled at her. "Leslie's watching us," she whispered to Ellen, who was petting her dog.

"I definitely know her secret," Ellen said slowly. "But first, I have a riddle for *her*."

Miss Hershey left the line to talk to another teacher.

"Get Leslie in line with us," Abby whispered.

"OK," Dunkum said. "I'll get her."

Soon Leslie came running over.

"Ellen says she knows your secret," Abby chanted.

Leslie put her hands on her hips. "Really?"

Ellen coughed. "Who is the mother of Jesus?"

Leslie looked puzzled. "Everybody knows that. What does Mary in the Bible have to do with my secret?"

"Who was Mary in the Christmas play at Grace Church two years ago?"

Leslie's face went white. "How should I know?" she stuttered.

"Because *you* were Mary in the Christmas play," said Ellen.

"How do you know that?" Leslie asked.

"I have a good memory," Ellen replied.

"But you didn't see me, did you?" said Leslie.

"No, but I heard you say your lines," said Ellen. "So did my cousin, Dunkum."

"Really?" Leslie asked. "You remember my voice?"

"I sure do," Ellen said.

Abby could not picture the mother of Jesus with stubby pigtails.

"You're right," said Leslie. "I was Mary. But that's not my secret. What else do you know about me?"

Ellen said, "Well, you had a different last name then."

Abby started adding up the clues. She checked them off in her head.

1. Miss Hershey winked at Leslie.

2. Leslie stayed inside with Miss Hershey during recess.

3. She moved her desk close to Miss Hershey's.

4. Miss Hershey knew Leslie's secret.

5. Miss Hershey owed Leslie money. She knew where Leslie's coin purse was.

6. Miss Hershey grabbed Leslie's hand during the fire alarm.

Abby thought it over and over. Like a good detective. She scratched her head. The clues all led to one person—their teacher.

"I've got it!" Abby shouted. "You're Miss Hershey's niece or cousin or something!"

Eric said, "No way! Leslie doesn't look anything like Miss Hershey."

"Maybe she's adopted," Stacy suggested.

Leslie looked surprised. "That's it! All of you are right."

"We are?" said Stacy, grinning.

There were some unanswered questions. Like any super sleuth, Abby refused to leave any loose ends.

"Why is your last name Groff and not Hershey?" Abby asked.

"I made up the name Groff," Leslie said, giggling. "Just for today."

"What about your father? Is he really a king?" Abby demanded.

"Oh, that," said Leslie. "I wanted to lead you astray."

"I knew it!" Abby said. "You tricked us on purpose."

Eric objected. "But that wasn't a fair clue."

"Clues are clues," said Leslie. "Some lead you off the track."

Abby wished Leslie were nicer about the whole thing.

"Why doesn't Dunkum remember Leslie?" Abby asked Ellen.

"Well, he should have ... because *he*

was Joseph!" Ellen laughed. "I told you Dunkum is forgetful!"

Abby and Stacy laughed. Dunkum didn't seem to mind. He leaped up and pretended to shoot a basket.

Jason wasn't laughing. He was staring at Leslie. He was frowning hard.

Just then, two fire trucks roared up.

"They're too late," said Dunkum. "Look!"

Coming out the back door, the principal carried a fire extinguisher. She held it high over her head.

The kids' cheering echoed around the playground.

Soon the "all clear" bell sounded. The kids filed inside.

Outside the classroom door, Jason pulled Abby aside. "You've got to help me," he whispered.

Jason's face was as white as a sheet!

TEN

"What's wrong with you, Jason?" Abby asked.

"Leslie's mad at me. That's what." Jason stopped. "And I've been mean to her. And . . ."

Abby looked at her watch. "And there's only fifteen minutes left of school today. What can you do to patch things up?" she asked.

"Think of something, will you?" Jason pleaded.

"I'll try." Abby couldn't think of much.

The kids took their seats, and Leslie whispered something to Miss Hershey.

Miss Hershey looked surprised. Then she put her hands on Leslie's shoulders. "Class, I am happy to introduce my niece to you. Her name is Leslie *Hershey*. She tells me you are all very good detectives."

The kids cheered. "Yahoo!"

Jason put his head down.

"What clues helped you most?" their teacher asked.

Abby raised her hand. "When you grabbed Leslie's hand during the fire alarm. That's something an aunt would probably do."

Stacy shot her hand up. "Leslie didn't come out for recess. If my aunt was the teacher, I might stay in and help her, too."

"Yeah, and she moved her desk next to yours," added Eric.

"But she doesn't look like you, Miss Hershey," said Dunkum. "That was real tricky!"

Miss Hershey smiled. "Leslie has been out of school for teacher work days. I wanted her to visit my class. But it was Leslie's idea to keep her identity a secret.

Was it good practice for solving mysteries?"

"Yes!" cried the class. Everyone clapped. Except Jason.

"Can we solve another mystery sometime?" Abby asked. She *loved* mysteries.

"That's a good idea. But now it's time to announce this week's Special Person."

Miss Hershey took a large candy bar from her desk drawer. The Special Person would be eating it soon! "Jason Birchall, you're the Special Person this week."

Jason sat up tall at his desk. "Thanks, Miss Hershey." He took the candy bar and popped it into his shirt pocket.

Miss Hershey reminded him to bring baby pictures and family pictures. And a list of his favorite things: books, games, and people. For the bulletin board.

Jason's favorite thing to do was *not* a secret. He liked to pig out on food. Mostly junk food.

Suddenly, Abby knew how to help Jason settle things with Leslie. But did she have time to tell him before the bell rang?

Quickly, she printed a note. Jason must *not* eat the candy bar in his pocket!

Jason scrunched his face into a frown when he read the note. He stared at Abby. "Why not?" he mouthed.

"Trust me," she mouthed back.

Rrrinng! The final bell.

Miss Hershey made an announcement. "Leslie will return to her own school tomorrow," she said. "Maybe she can come back for another visit sometime."

The kids called good-bye to Leslie.

Abby rushed to Jason's desk. "Hurry or you'll be too late." She glanced at Leslie. She was cleaning out her desk.

"What should I do?" Jason whined.

Abby tapped on the candy bar through his shirt pocket. The apple seeds were still in there, too. "Here's your answer," she said. "If you want to win her over, give her your candy bar."

Jason sighed. "How do you know it'll work?"

"Remember the Golden Rule? Treat others the way you want to be treated. Leslie *loves* sweets."

"That makes two of us." Slowly, he pulled the candy bar out of its hiding place. He held it in his hand. "I shouldn't eat this," he said sadly. "It cancels out the good stuff I had for lunch."

He held the candy bar to his nose. He breathed deeply. "Smells great," he said with glazed eyes. Then he saw the teacher's niece packing her things.

"Better decide now," Abby said. "She's on her way home."

Leslie and Miss Hershey walked out the door and into the hallway.

"Leslie, wait!" Jason called.

Leslie stopped. She looked surprised. Turning to her aunt, she said, "Go ahead. I'll catch up in a second."

Abby watched from the door. She heard Jason say he was sorry about chasing Leslie. Then he offered her the candy bar.

Abby held her breath. *Please be nice, Leslie.*

Leslie raised her eyebrows. She looked embarrassed. "Thanks," Leslie said quietly. "You're A-OK!"

Jason took a deep breath. "You're OK, too." He paused.

Now what? thought Abby.

"Uh, you can call me a show-off if you want to."

"So . . . we're friends?" Leslie said, smiling.

"Friends," he said.

Then Leslie unwrapped the candy bar and gave him half. "Show-off isn't the best name for you," Leslie said. She pulled on her pigtails. "Sharing is much better."

Jason turned bright red.

Abby wished she had a camera. This was a perfect picture for the Special Person bulletin board. She hurried off to tell Stacy.

"Hey, Abby, wait up!" Jason called to her.

Abby laughed. She pretended to take his picture.

"Don't be silly." Jason held out his half

of the candy bar. "Want a bite?"

Abby reached for it.

"Happy School Spirit Day!" he shouted, taking it back. In one bite it was gone.

Abby wasn't finished with Jason. She had a great idea. "Race you home."

"I'm too tired," Jason said, munching.

"I have a feeling my mom made brownies," she said, starting to run.

Jason's eyes grew wide. He rubbed his stomach. He took off after Abby.

Abby raced across the playground to Blossom Hill Lane.

The Cul-de-sac Kids cheered as Jason ran all the way to Abby's porch. He collapsed on the steps. "OK, now let's have those brownies!"

"Just kidding," Abby shouted. "Happy School Spirit Day!"

Jason burst into laughter.

Abby wished School Spirit Day were closer than a whole year away.

The Cul-de-Sac Kids Series

Don't Miss #24!

THE MIDNIGHT MYSTERY

Dunkum's end-of-school party turns into a huge mystery. His cousin's guide dog, Honey, is suddenly missing after the celebration. At midnight!

Feeling responsible, Dunkum gets some help from the Cul-de-sac Kids. Abby Hunter and the others play detective along with Dunkum. But it's not all fun and games.

Who'd want to steal Ellen's beloved dog in the first place? What will happen if Dunkum doesn't unravel the mystery? It's the dognapping adventure of the year!

About the Author

Beverly Lewis first got the idea for this story from her schoolteacher sister. Barbara Birch played a trick on her fourth grade class. Beverly wanted to write about the real-life trick. So she wrote *The Upside-Down Day* to share the fun—the mystery, too—with her many chapter book readers.

"Did *you* guess Leslie's secret along with Abby Hunter?" asks Beverly.

Even if you don't have a mystery student in your class, you could have a school spirit day this year.

The Cul-de-sac Kids series offers adventure, mystery, and fun. Be sure to collect each book!

Learn more about Beverly and her books at *www.BeverlyLewis.com*

Also by Beverly Lewis

Adult Nonfiction

Amish Prayers
The Beverly Lewis Amish Heritage Cookbook

Adult Fiction

HOME TO HICKORY HOLLOW

The Fiddler • *The Bridesmaid* • *The Guardian* • *The Secret Keeper* • *The Last Bride*

SEASONS OF GRACE

The Secret • *The Missing* • *The Telling*

ABRAM'S DAUGHTERS

The Covenant • *The Betrayal* • *The Sacrifice* • *The Prodigal* • *The Revelation*

ANNIE'S PEOPLE

The Preacher's Daughter • *The Englisher* • *The Brethren*

THE ROSE TRILOGY

The Thorn • *The Judgment* • *The Mercy*

THE COURTSHIP OF NELLIE FISHER

The Parting • *The Forbidden* • *The Longing*

THE HERITAGE OF LANCASTER COUNTY

The Shunning • *The Confession* • *The Reckoning*

OTHER ADULT FICTION

The Postcard • *The Crossroad* • *The Redemption of Sarah Cain*
October Song • *Sanctuary** • *The Sunroom* • *Child of Mine**
The River • *The Love Letters* • *The Photograph*

Youth Fiction

Girls Only (GO!) Volume One and *Volume Two*†
SummerHill Secrets Volume One and *Volume Two*‡
Holly's Heart Collection One†, *Collection Two*‡, and *Collection Three*†

www.BeverlyLewis.com

* with David Lewis   † 4 books in each volume   ‡ 5 books in each volume